Everest

By Jim Howes

PM Nonfiction
part of the Rigby PM Collection

U.S. edition © 2001 Rigby
a division of Reed Elsevier Inc.
1000 Hart Road
Barrington, IL 60010–2627
www.rigby.com

Text © Nelson Thomson Learning 2001
Illustrations © Nelson Thomson Learning 2001
Originally published in Australia by Nelson Thomson Learning

06 05 04 03 02
10 9 8 7 6 5 4 3 2

Everest
ISBN 0 7578 1167 1

Designed by Karen Mayo
Photographs by Australian Picture Library/Corbis, p. 16 top; Australian Picture Library/
Corbis/AFP, p. 25; Australian Picture Library/Corbis/Brian Vikander, p. 14 left; Australian
Picture Library/Corbis/Christine Kolish, p. 9; Australian Picture Library/Corbis/Galen Rowell,
pp. 1, 6-7 background, 10 inset, 11 top, 20 and back cover, 20-21 background and cover,
24-25 background, 30; Australian Picture Library/Corbis/Hulton-Deutsch Collection, p. 26;
Australian Picture Library/Corbis/John Noble, pp. 8-9 background; Australian Picture Library/
Corbis/Paul A. Souders, p. 19; Coo-ee Picture Library, p. 29 (newspaper); Eric Simonson,
p. 24; Jake Norton/Mountain World Photograph, pp. 2-3, 4-5, 10 background, 14 right,
32-33; John P Stevens/The Ancient Art & Architecture Collection, pp. 4-5 center; Royal
Geographical Society, pp. 12, 13 right, 16 bottom, 17 top and bottom and cover 18, 22 top
and bottom, 23, 27, 28, 29 and cover; The Photo Library-Sydney/Michael Bennetts, p. 31;
The Science Museum/Science & Society Picture Library, p. 13 left; William B Sykes/
The Ancient Art & Architecture Collection, pp. 4-5 front.

Printed in China by Midas Printing (Asia) Ltd

Contents

The Lure of the Mountain

"Because it's there."

George Mallory, mountaineer, answering the question, "Why do you want climb Mount Everest?," 1921

People have always been fascinated by mountains. Mountains have influenced the lives of people from cultures all over the world. They have inspired storytellers, poets, and artists. They have challenged scientists, adventurers, and dreamers.

Mountains capture our imagination. Even architecture tends to imitate a mountain's shape. Just look at the great pyramids of ancient Egypt, or the temples of the Mayans in Central America. These great structures and buildings reflect a mountain's shape.

Mount Everest, on the border of Nepal and Tibet, is the tallest mountain on Earth. People are drawn to it for all sorts of reasons and with all sorts of results.

Pyramids and temples imitate a mountain's shape

5

The 60 Million-Year-Old Challenge

India

"The wind is the appalling enemy.
It is mind-destroying, physically
destroying, and soul-destroying."

Chris Bonnington, Everest mountaineer, 1975

Asia

The Himalayan Stretch

The Himalayan mountain range is 1,500 miles long. It is the youngest mountain range on Earth.

If you stood on Mount Everest, you would be standing on the highest point of land on Earth. If jumbo jets were to fly over the summit at their normal **altitude**, a climber at the top could wave to passengers through the windows.

The Himalayan mountain range, which Mount Everest is part of, has most of the tallest mountain peaks in the world. Mount Everest, measured in 1999 using **global-positioning satellites**, is 29,032 feet above sea level.

Mount Everest was formed about 60 million years ago. As Earth's continents drifted apart, the land mass that is now India collided with the greater land mass that is now Asia. When the two lands met, the impact forced part of the land downward and the rest upward, forming the mountain range of the Himalayas. The Himalayas took millions of years to form. Scientists tell us that even today, the mountain range is still shifting.

The Culture of the Mountain

"The Goddess of the Sky is both love and destruction."

Buddhist monk

Mount Everest has always been important to local cultures. Tucked away on the border of Nepal and Tibet, Mount Everest is known to the Nepalese as Chomolungma *(cho-mo-loong-ma)* which means "mother goddess of the universe." In Tibet, it is known as Sagarmatha *(sa-gar-math-a),* which means "goddess of the sky."

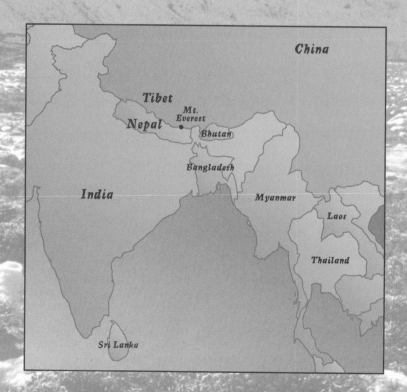

Mount Everest has been sacred to Nepalese and Tibetan people for thousands of years. They believed that the mountain peak was to be respected from a distance, rather than climbed. Even so, the Sherpas of Nepal were famous mountain climbers, long before Tenzing Norgay and Edmund Hillary conquered the peak in 1953.

Himalayan Tiger

The word *Sherpa* is used to describe the Nepalese people who live high in the Himalayas. It means *tiger*.

Today, the mountains are still sacred to the Himalayan people, and they climb them reluctantly. The Sherpas of Nepal are regarded as the best guides and climbers to have when attempting to reach the high summits. The number of foreign climbing expeditions has increased so much in recent years that many Sherpas now depend on this tourist trade for their income.

Sherpas preparing to climb

Climbing Ceremony

Every peak in the Himalaya region is sacred, so mountain climbers must prepare for their expeditions by performing a ceremony with the local Sherpas. This ceremony is usually held at Base Camp, the camp from which the attempt to climb Mount Everest is organized.

During the ceremony, models of the mountains are made from barley flour. The climbers throw handfuls of rice into the air, and multicolored **prayer flags** are strung out from high poles. The small mountain models are blessed and the prayer flags flap in the wind, carrying prayers to the mountains. Once the ceremony is complete, the climbers may proceed.

Preparing the barley flour mountains for the ceremony

Mapping the Mountain

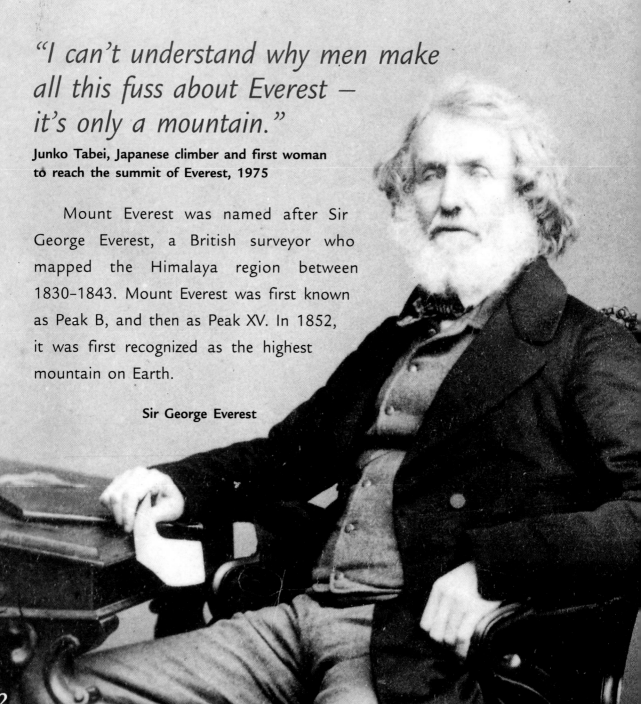

"I can't understand why men make all this fuss about Everest — it's only a mountain."

Junko Tabei, Japanese climber and first woman to reach the summit of Everest, 1975

Mount Everest was named after Sir George Everest, a British surveyor who mapped the Himalaya region between 1830–1843. Mount Everest was first known as Peak B, and then as Peak XV. In 1852, it was first recognized as the highest mountain on Earth.

Sir George Everest

But most of the world learned about Mount Everest much later than 1852 because information about the Himalaya region was difficult to obtain. Finally, in 1892, a member of a British survey office announced that he had completed all calculations collected over the years, and had officially discovered the highest mountain in the world.

During the early 1800s, information about the height of Everest and the surrounding region was gathered by the British from a distance of almost 200 miles away! They used large, heavy mapping devices that needed 12 men to carry them.

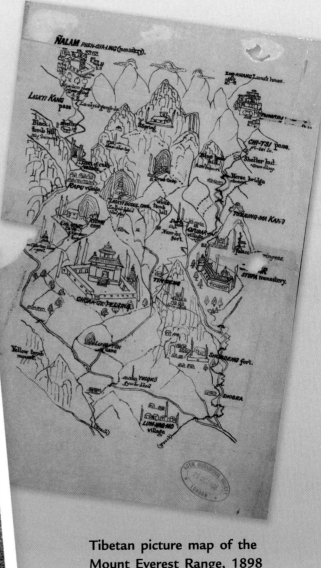

Tibetan picture map of the
Mount Everest Range, 1898

This huge measuring device, used in 1849, established
Mount Everest as the highest mountain in the world.

In the second half of the 1800s, some of the methods used to measure Mount Everest and the surrounding mountains were extraordinary. The British put together a team whose secret mission was to sneak into Tibet and Nepal and take measurements.

The men in this team were Indians, and they disguised themselves as monks, travelers, or merchants. They spent months exploring the region and taking secret notes. Scientific instruments were not allowed on this secret mission — they would attract attention. So the team had to use other methods to get accurate measurements.

The team measured altitude by boiling water. They knew that water reached its boiling point at a lower temperature in higher altitudes. So they noted the water's temperature when it was boiling and calculated their altitude. They carried their notes and maps inside hollow walking-sticks, **prayer cylinders,** or arm bracelets.

Secret information was carried out of Nepal and Tibet in prayer cylinders (below) and arm bracelets (right).

14

The end result was that Everest was discovered to be the highest peak in the world. And by the early 1900s, people were talking seriously about trying to climb it, even though it was thousands of feet higher than any mountain previously climbed. The British were determined to be the first to succeed in what they considered the last great conquering challenge — climbing Mount Everest.

167°F at 26,000 feet above sea level.

188°F at 13,000 feet above sea level.

Water boils at a lower temperature in higher altitudes. Altitude was calculated by boiling water at various points on the mountains.

212°F at sea level.

Early Climbing on Everest

"We are about to walk off the map."

George Mallory, climber and explorer

Attempting to climb the world's tallest mountain was very difficult. Some climbers thought Mount Everest could *never* be climbed because they believed that people could not survive in altitudes above 23,000 feet.

George Mallory

In 1921, a British expedition explored and mapped the Nepalese region around Mount Everest. George Mallory was one of the leaders of this expedition. He was an expert mountain climber and had climbed several high-altitude mountains. This expedition influenced his decision, three years later, to climb Mount Everest.

The British attempted to climb Mount Everest in 1922 and 1924. These attempts were extremely difficult because of inappropriate clothing and equipment. The clothing worn by early climbers offered little protection against the freezing conditions. The equipment carried was heavy and cumbersome.

Preparing to climb Mount Everest, 1921

Oxygen at High Altitude

Oxygen is important for climbers at high altitudes. It helps maintain energy levels and creates much needed body heat. But there is little oxygen in the air at altitudes over 26,000 feet. Breathing is difficult, and as a result, every movement is hard to perform. The early climbers carried oxygen cylinders to increase their oxygen intake. But these cylinders were very heavy to carry, making climbing even more difficult.

Equipment and clothing have improved over time. Yet, even with modern equipment, climbers today still face the serious challenges of weather, **fatigue**, and danger. The task of climbing Mount Everest over seventy years ago must have been enormous.

Early oxygen apparatus, the sort used by Mallory and Irvine

Wind Chill

Temperatures on Everest are low, but the real cold comes from the wind. The wind can reach 50–100 miles per hour — strong enough to blow climbers off their feet! It creates wind chills of -75°F, or even lower.

What Climbers Wore in 1924

Woolen hat

Goggles

3 oxygen cylinders, weighing 33 lbs each

Woolen gloves

Jacket made out of heavy wool

A windproof smock made out of woven cotton or linen

Puttees: long cloth wound around the lower leg for warmth

Sweaters and shirts made out of wool

Single boots worn with 3–4 socks. Leather soles with nails to aid grip

Ice axe: made out of heavy steel, weighing about 4 lbs

18

What Climbers Wear Today

Light woolen hat worn under hood of jacket

2–4 oxygen cylinders, weighing 4 lbs each

Goggles and a face mask

Gloves under heavy mittens

Ice axe: made from special metal, weighing about 2 lbs

Long thermal underwear

Pants and a down-filled body suit with hood

A radio to keep in touch with team members and to report any problems

Double boots

An Extreme World

"I was in continual agony. I have never in my life been so tired as on the summit of Everest that day. I just sat there, oblivious to everything."

Reinhold Messner, 1978, first to climb Everest without the aid of extra oxygen

The "Death Zone"

Climbers, hoping to reach the summit of Mount Everest, have created new terms such as the "death zone" — the name given to the zone above 26,000 feet. At this altitude, the amount of oxygen in the air is about half the amount many of us are used to. Body cells become starved of oxygen and begin to cease functioning.

Lack of Oxygen

The last part of the climb up Mount Everest is a race against time. Climbers have to reach the peak and then climb down before any damage to their bodies becomes permanent.

Climbers in the death zone suffer extreme **dehydration**. The blood thickens and extra water is needed to thin the blood to aid circulation. Climbers must drink about five or six quarts of water a day.

The lack of oxygen to the brain also creates risks. The brain ceases to function properly and climbers can experience **delusions** and make wrong decisions. A wrong decision can be fatal. Climbers are trained to recognize symptoms such as personality change, loss of memory, and brain damage early, and to take protective action.

Altitude Sickness

"Then, on the way up toward the summit, I stood out on the very edge and I was sure that if I had jumped off from that point, I could have flown... Somewhere came this thought that, you know, Peter, maybe you're not thinking quite right.

And I had to literally bite my cheek to draw blood and hit my face. I took off my oxygen mask, hit my face and slapped my head around and started to come out of it."

Peter Hackett climbed solo to Everest in 1981. He is an Affiliate Professor of Medicine at the University of Washington in Seattle.

Off the Mountain, into Legend

> ## "I can't see myself coming down defeated."
>
> **George Mallory, before his fatal climbing attempt on Everest in 1924**

On June 6, 1924, George Mallory and Andrew Irvine left their fellow climbers to complete the final stages of climbing Mount Everest. They were part of a large, well-organized expedition. Mallory and Irvine were determined to enter the history books that day.

Base Camp at Everest

Mallory and Irvine were an interesting pair. Mallory was regarded as a brilliant climber. He had many years of climbing experience. Irvine was much younger and less experienced, but they climbed beautifully together, with speed and an easy rhythm.

Andrew Irvine at Base Camp, 1924

Dear John,

We'll probably start early tomorrow (8th) in order to have clear weather. It won't be too early to start looking for us either crossing the rock band under the pyramid or going up the skyline at 8:00 P.M.

Yours ever,
G. Mallory

Mallory (left) and Irvine (right) preparing for their assault on the summit

On June 8, 1924, the day of the final climb to the summit, Mallory wrote two notes. One was to Captain John Noel, the expedition's cameraman who was going to film their assault on the summit from a lower camp.

Mallory meant *8:00* A.M., not 8:00 P.M. Back then, no climber would head up to the summit at night! The aim was always to get up and back before dark.

The other note was to team member, Noel Odell. Mallory reported his and Irvine's oxygen supply and what they intended to do. He also apologized for the mess they had left in the camp.

As Mallory and Irvine were climbing, the rest of the team in the lower camp performed their duties. Odell, a geologist, searched for and found the first fossils on Mount Everest. At 12:50 P.M., he stopped and looked up toward the summit where his friends were climbing.

The clouds cleared and he saw two tiny black dots moving quickly near the summit. Odell estimated they were within 800 feet of the summit.

Then the mist rolled in and Mallory and Irvine were hidden. They were never seen by their team members again.

A Mystery Uncovered

Since that day, their story has been kept alive by researchers, other climbers, and the media. What happened to Mallory and Irvine? Did they reach the summit? Did they die on their way up or down the mountain?

Seventy-five years later, in 1999, a research team traveled the same route to the top of Mount Everest as Mallory and Irvine. They were determined to find their bodies. The team hoped that either Mallory or Irvine carried a camera. If they had reached the summit, surely a photograph would show it.

The research team that found Mallory, 1999

The team discovered Mallory's body. Several pieces of equipment and clothing were found, along with a discarded oxygen cylinder. Returning home with these clues, the research team pieced together the last day Mallory and Irvine had spent on the mountain. They suggest that Mallory and Irvine did reach the summit of Everest that day — almost thirty years before the official first successful climb.

Perhaps when Irvine's body is found, a camera might be with it. Then the world will know for sure.

Mallory's oxygen cylinder, found 1999

Mallory Found

The 1999 research expedition discovered Mallory's body as well as one of Mallory and Irvine's oxygen cylinders.

Mallory's body was face down, in a **scree slope**. He had fallen. His right leg was broken and lay at a strange angle across his left. He had broken ribs and a broken elbow. His hands were dug deep into the stones.

When the team had finished gathering their evidence, they gave Mallory a long-overdue funeral — no doubt the highest service ever held.

Victory on Everest

"As far as I knew, he had never taken a photograph before, and the summit of Everest was hardly the place to show him how."

Edmund Hillary, talking about taking a photo of Tenzing Norgay

In 1952, the British put together a team that they believed could not fail to reach the top of Everest. After months of planning, the attempt was made in 1953, as a celebration of the coronation of the new British queen, Elizabeth II.

John Hunt led the expedition. He approached this task with precision. He chose a team that had specific skills, or skills that complemented those of the other team members. A climbing strategy was worked out. Extra camps at high altitudes were created, giving support to climbers attempting the final summit. The best equipment in the world was available for the expedition.

The expedition had enough support and equipment for two attempts on the summit, by two different pairs of climbers. Oxygen was required for all climbing in the upper regions.

Edmund Hillary, a New Zealander with a reputation for strength and endurance, and head Sherpa, Tenzing Norgay, were part of this team.

Edmund Hillary

Tenzing Norgay

The First Attempt

After reaching the final camp, preparations were made for the first attempt. Two climbers, Evans and Bourdillon, struggled with the oxygen equipment. They had to turn back after reaching the second summit, about 650 feet lower than the top. Evans and Bourdillon had climbed to 28,000 feet. This was a world record — no one had officially reached that height and returned successfully before.

Evans and Bourdillon return, exhausted, from their attempt on the summit

The 1953 Everest expedition team members

27

The Second Attempt

For a couple of days, strong winds made any further attempts to reach the summit impossible. Then, on May 28, Hillary and Tenzing Norgay set out with their support party. At 27,800 feet, the support team left supplies with them, and returned to a lower camp.

That night, Hillary and Tenzing Norgay camped on a small, sloping ledge. They opened an oxygen cylinder inside the tent to help them breathe and keep warm.

The next morning, at 6:30 A.M., Hillary and Tenzing Norgay left for the summit. By 9:00 A.M., they had reached the same point where their two teammates had been forced to turn back only two days earlier. Steep, rocky surfaces rose before them. The pair worked quickly and effectively, one roped to the other, moving up the mountain with smoothness and harmony.

Finally, Hillary and Tenzing Norgay were on the snowy dome of the summit. A few feet more and they were on the top of the world. It was 11:30 A.M. on May 29, 1953.

Hillary looked toward the area where Mallory and Irvine had disappeared, and wondered. Tenzing Norgay made offerings to the gods of Chomolungma. But there was no time to loiter — they had to return to the protection of their camp before dark. It was now almost noon. Hillary took a photograph of Tenzing Norgay on the summit and then they left. The world's highest mountain now had human footprints on its uppermost peak.

> "I have climbed my mountain, but I still must live my life."
>
> Tenzing Norgay

Tenzing Norgay
on the summit of
Mount Everest, 1953

Crowded Mountain

"Chomolungma is our mother.
She gives us our lives and our dreams."
Buddhist monk

The number of people who have now reached the top of Mount Everest might well be close to 1,000. People have successfully climbed Everest solo and without oxygen. Even people who have never mountain climbed before have reached the summit. Commercial tour companies now take up novice climbers. The mountain is crowded. Routes discovered by the first climbers are now often traveled. Solitude is hard to find.

Climbers report that trash litters the climbing paths. Climbers Reinhold Messner and Peter Habeler, the first men to reach the summit without using oxygen cylinders, left nothing behind on the mountain. These climbers didn't use bolts to fix ropes since that would have meant leaving the bolts behind.

Even the research team that found Mallory's body had problems when climbers became entangled in an old rope left by earlier climbers.

Oxygen bottles and old tents are scattered over the mountain. There is even an old helicopter wreck left by an Italian team when they crashed there in 1978.

The environmental impact that climbers have created on Mount Everest may one day be reversed — but the impact of Mount Everest on climbers and the human race will last forever.

Cleaning up Mount Everest;
a climber picks up a
discarded oxygen cylinder

Glossary

altitude the vertical height of an object above sea level

dehydration not having enough water in your body

delusions mistaken ideas or thoughts

fatigue extreme tiredness, exhaustion

global-positioning satellites satellites that can take accurate measurements of objects on Earth

prayer cylinders cylinders, or wheels, that are inscribed with prayers

prayer flags flags that are inscribed with prayers

scree slope a rocky slope at the foot of a hill or cliff